Sour Milk

A Short, Sharp Horror Shock

Morgan Delaney

Published by Morgan Delaney

www.morgandelaney.info

Contact: morgan@morgandelaney.info

Edited by Joe Nassise

Cover design by MiblArt

Sour Milk/ Morgan Delaney. —1st, 2nd ebook ed. 2020, 3rd ebook ed. 2021

Sour Milk/ Morgan Delaney. —1st print ed. 2021

Print ISBN 978-3-98566-004-9

Contents

For Nadine.
My one and only.

One

LEE HARDLY SLEPT before being dragged out of bed. He washed in icy water with the other children before they filed into the classroom. The morning was overcast. Drizzle spat at the windows. The white paint looked grey, black in the corners where mould climbed the walls. Lee sat in the front row, listening to the snuffled breathing behind him. The room smelled of chalk and damp. At the window nearest the teacher's desk stood a life-sized shop window dummy wearing a wide, dark brown woollen suit and black boots. With the light behind it, it was hard to tell, but Lee felt it was watching them. He needed the toilet, but didn't dare raise his hand.

A woman sat at the front of the classroom. The policeman had called her Miss Dunn in his soft Galway accent when he delivered Lee to The Lambs of Our Lord Children's Home the previous day. Her mouth had curled down when she saw him. Now she was calling someone. "Ivan?" Lee sniffed at his jumper. It smelled of the policeman's cigarettes. Miss Dunn called again. "Ivan?" The policeman had called the orphanage "the Lamb's Home" on the drive down and Lee had imagined a cottage among green fields. "Ivan?" Lee looked around. All the other children had their eyes downcast. "Ivan?" She was staring at Lee, her pen poised over a jotter on her desk. Lee felt himself blush with embarrassment at the attention. The policeman had told her his name. Had she made a mistake? "Ivan?" She picked up a metre-stick and rose. The dummy rocked as she brushed past. "No, thank you," she said. "I shall manage this." She stopped beside Lee. "Ivan?" She bent over him, her breath smelling of sour milk.

"Please, Missus, my name is—"

"Ivan!" She whipped the metre-stick across his fingers on the desk and turned back to continue the roll call. The dummy rocked again as the children answered in turn when she looked at them: all of them an Ivan or an Anna. His fingers aching, Lee kept his eyes on the dummy by the window. It had realistic rubber hands but only a ball of wood the colour of dried wheat for a head. Two lines were carved into it for eyes. He had been told that its name was Mr Leonard and that it would get him.

Two

"NEW CHILDREN should introduce themselves, Ivan," said Miss Dunn.

Lee clamped his jaws together. "Yes, Missus. My name is—"

"Ivan." She paced back towards him, fixing him with her eyes, huge behind her glasses. "Why are you here?"

"Please, Missus, they sent me here," he said.

"Of course you were sent here. No one chooses Corkragh, don't be facetious." A snigger from the back of the class somewhere.

"Please, Missus, they sent me because I have no parents," said Lee. The words caught in his throat. He kept his eyes down.

"Are they dead?"

"Yes, Missus."

"Then say: 'They're dead.'"

"Yes, Missus."

"An accident?"

"Yes, Missus."

"Was it?"

"Yes, Missus."

"Ivan?"

The dummy—Mr Leonard—leaned in closer.

"Was it?"

"Car accident. Missus."

Miss Dunn waited.

"My mother was killed in a car accident, Missus."

"Ah! And your father?"

"My father is also dead, Missus."

"Car accident." She walked around him.

"No, Missus. My father died before, Missus."

"How?"

"He was ill, Missus."

"Ill?"

"Yes, Missus."

"'Yes, Missus?'"

"He was ill, and he died, Missus."

She shook her head. "He killed himself, Ivan. It wasn't an accident."

Lee said nothing.

"'Yes, Missus?'" said Miss Dunn. "'Yes, Missus?' Your father killed himself and your mother decided she'd rather be dead than look after you on her own. 'Yes, Missus?' And nobody else wanted you, so now you're my problem. 'Yes, Missus?'"

"… yes, Missus," said Lee. He held onto his desk, fingers scratching at a corner.

She bent to look him straight in the eyes. "It's 'Miss,'" she spat into his face. Lee twitched. She grabbed his ear, biting into the flesh of the lobe with a red thumbnail.

"Put your hand out," she said.

He put out his left hand. His right hand was still sore.

"The other one," she said.

Lee hesitated, then put out his right hand, its knuckles still swollen.

"Never lie to me. Ivan!" She held the metre-stick above her head, then whipped it across his hand. She walked back to her desk, disappearing into the cloud of chalk dust raised by the metre-stick, leaving Lee at his desk with his eyes screwed up.

"Mr Leonard, you may start the lesson."

Three

AFTER CLASSES, the children were expected to clean the orphanage. One girl, Noreen, filled a tray with food and brought it upstairs to Miss Dunn. Another girl divided up the rest of the work. She had fine worry lines around her eyes and forehead, though she couldn't have been much older than Lee. She gave him the job of cleaning the kitchen with Gareth, the boy he had sat with in class, and Ross, who had told him that Mr Leonard would get him. The ashes needed to be raked out of the Aga stove and the plates washed and dried and put away. Every surface needed to be cleaned and dusted. The floor had to be swept and mopped. The girl disappeared into the scullery with some of the others to do the never—ending laundry.

It was dark before they could eat. Two pots of boiled, salted potatoes to share among them all and a cup of watered-down milk each. It had gone off. They called it buttermilk.

The girl with the worry lines sat across from Lee. "I'm Josey," she said. "But Dunn calls all the girls 'Anna.'" She pointed to the boy he had sat beside in class. "This is Gareth, but 'Ivan,' when Dunn is around. Don't forget. When she calls, you just watch her eyes to see who she means."

"I'm Lee," he said. He was scrawny, with a caved-in chest, large head and nose. It made him look innocent, almost stupid. And much too soft. Dunn would make short work of him.

◆

Sunday was a good day. The children were allowed out in the sunshine. There was an early spring chill in the air, but the sun warmed them. They sucked in deep breaths, feasting on the sweet scent of chlorophyll, happy to be away from the mushroomy smell of the orphanage. Josey had the smaller children pretend the chilled air was ice-cream. They closed their eyes and sucked in deep breaths, imagining the air was soft and creamy, laden with white sugar crystals and juicy red berries. They stayed in the front garden as the high hedges surrounding the orphanage kept the rest of the grounds in permanent shade, the earth a drab field, brown under swollen moss.

The grass was over-long after winter and the hedges were ragged. Josey used the pretext of adjusting the buckle on her worn sandals to run her fingers through the cool grass. She wrapped a blade around her index finger and pulled, feeling the wet smack as it ripped. The girls were admiring the sprouting buds in the box hedge. The boys were eating the catkins on the alder tree, despite the bitter taste.

When Miss Dunn appeared in the doorway, the children quietened and looked out over the hedge to the road. There was little to see. The orphanage, an old converted manor house, lay two miles out of town surrounded by a bog. A single lane track wound its way past the gate. Passersby were rare, mainly men on their way to cut turf and with no interest in children. But the view—away from the orphanage—was coveted. Visitors to the orphanage were rare.

◆

In the evening, after they had washed, the children lined up outside the washroom, in case Miss Dunn came to inspect them. Josey could hear voices coming from Miss Dunn's apartment. The radio. "Or Mr Leonard," said Noreen. They waited. Eventually, Josey told them to get to bed. She looked around the single bedroom that they all shared before switching off the light. A few of the beds were empty. Ross's bed, Enda and Terry's beds. Lee's.

Josey tip-toed back to the washroom to listen.

"Can you hear me, Ivan?" It was Ross's voice, followed by a slap.

She ran back to get Gareth. Ross was almost as old as Gareth, which is to say nearly old enough to leave the orphanage, but much smaller. His triangular face made him look younger, too. Miss Dunn let him get away with more than the other children, as he was useful. He and Noreen helped her keep the others under control.

When Josey returned with Gareth, Ross was with Enda and Terry around one of the farthest sinks. It was full of water. Terry held Lee's arms while Ross pushed his head under water.

"Ivan? Can you hear me, Ivan?" said Ross.

Lee coughed and choked as he tried to suck in air. Gareth ran at them, and Ross skidded backwards, falling on the floor. The others backed away. Josey grabbed Lee.

"Wanker," shouted Ross. Gareth kicked him in the chest.

Ross held himself and scowled. "He needs to learn his name," he said. "He'll get us all in trouble."

Four

ROSS CORNERED LEE after class the next day. Miss Dunn had singled Lee out again, and his hands were so swollen from the lashing with the stick that he could barely touch anything. Enda dragged him into the orphanage's disused second classroom.

"Well, Ivan?" said Ross.

Lee said nothing.

"Answer me!" Ross waved a metre-stick through the air, barely missing Lee's face.

Lee turned when he heard a snigger. The tall girl was there, the one with the red cheeks. Noreen. Ross nodded to Enda, who pulled up Lee's shirt while Terry held him. When Lee kicked out, Terry lifted him easily, leaving his legs dangling stupidly. Noreen sniggered.

Ross swung the metre-stick two-handed at Lee's belly. It whipped against his stomach, cracking loudly. Lee's belly bloomed purplish-pink. He started to cry.

"Come on, Jelly-Belly, what's your name?" Ross lashed him again.Lee cried out, and Ross lashed him. Lee's belly was virulent purple, pinpricks of blood rising to the surface of the skin.

Ross lashed him twice more before Terry dropped him on the floor, where Lee lay doubled up.

"I'm only getting started, Ivan," said Ross. "Get up."

Ross kicked at him. "Get up, coward."

"… not a coward," said Lee.

"You're crying like a baby!" said Ross. "Course you're a coward."

Lee shook his head.

"Prove it," said Ross.

Lee looked up, unsure if this was another trick.

"Next time someone has detention you follow them," said Ross. "Then tell me you're not a coward."

Lee got to his feet and staggered from the room.

◆

"Ivan will show what he learned yesterday," said Miss Dunn. She stood in front of the blackboard, which she had filled the previous day without explaining what any of it meant. She looked at Lee. He was staring out the window. When she turned for the metre-stick propped against the wall, Gareth kicked him.

"Yes, Miss Dunn?" said Lee automatically. He had been miles away from the orphanage, but now his fingers throbbed.

"Yes. Now."

Lee stood, unsure what was required. Miss Dunn waited, ignoring a snigger. Mr Leonard had his back to them today as he inspected the sluggish weather.

She sighed theatrically. "We spent all of yesterday showing you what to do. Mr Leonard explained it. I demonstrated. Show me we're not wasting our time with another stupid child. Are you stupid?"

Lee walked to the board, already balling his hands up to protect them from the inevitable lash of the stick. The tree in the front garden rustled in the wind as he passed the window, trying to keep as much distance as possible between himself and Mr Leonard. Did he imagine it moved as he came closer?

He saw it. In the bottom corner was an incomplete equation, half-obscured by Mr Leonard's shadow. He picked up the chalk from its dusty bed, his numb fingers almost dropping it. A snigger. Miss Dunn whirled on the class, slamming the metre-stick across the nearest desk. Josey barely pulled her hand away in time. Chalk dust clouded the air as the crack echoed around the room, counterpoint to the scrape of the chalk as Lee completed the equation. He stepped back so Dunn could read it. Her face was expressionless. She nodded, and Lee moved back to his desk. The room seemed lighter, the atmosphere less oppressive. He glanced towards the window to see if the sun had come out. It hadn't. Some trick of the light, though, had made Lee think Mr Leonard was looking out into the garden. Now he could see the dummy was watching the class, staring over Lee's head to the back of the room.

◆

Noreen cleaned Miss Dunn's apartment. It was one of the easier chores but meant being alone with Miss Dunn, something most of the children wanted to avoid. The evening was mild, and Ross and Enda were outside cutting the grass. In the kitchen, Josey pulled out some paper she had hoarded.

"What are you doing?" asked Lee.

"How did you know the answer today?" answered Josey.

"They're easy," he said

The children gathered around the table, and Lee explained. He was shy at first but had always been clever and quickly became animated. "They're called equations because both sides should be equal. So that's what you do. Make both sides equal." He started explaining how to do it. When the staircase creaked, Josey gathered up the papers. Noreen came in, but they were already moving, cleaning up the kitchen.

◆

Siobhan was called first to the board the next day. Before Lee arrived, she had been Miss Dunn's favourite victim.

She stood at the board, caught in Miss Dunn's gaze. Mr Leonard was standing at the back of the classroom, which made it harder to ignore him. Lee couldn't check that the dummy wasn't staring at him. When Miss Dunn started to smile, Siobhan picked up the tiny piece of chalk and wrote. Her hand shook. She hacked the answer onto the board. She glanced back at Lee, who nodded. Siobhan waited. Miss Dunn followed her gaze to Lee, then nodded for her to sit.

"Anna." Miss Dunn pointed to Josey. Once she was at the board, the teacher stood directly behind her to block her view of Lee. Josey scribbled an answer. She stood back from the board before she could second guess herself and waited for Dunn to lash out.

"Sit," said Dunn. She spat it out and glared around the classroom.

"Ivan." She stood beside Lee. His jaw clenched. "Solve the last equation, Ivan."

Lee remained at his place. Lee. His name was Lee.

Dunn whispered her sour milk breath into his ear, loud enough for everyone to hear. "Even little Anna knows how to do this. No wonder your parents wanted to get away from you." She paused for a snigger from the back of the room, then lashed Lee across the spine. The hollow thump caused an indrawn breath in the classroom and stopped the snigger. Miss Dunn went back to her desk. "We can't move on until Ivan finishes the equation," she said. Lee shook with pain and the effort of not crying. She pulled out her blue damp-mottled jotter and wrote for the rest of the afternoon. Lee wondered if his back was bleeding. His back felt wet as it burned. Long after it had grown dark, she continued writing before finally pointing at Noreen, who lined the children up for the end of class.

"What do you say?" said Noreen.
"Thank you, Miss Dunn."

Five

"IVAN," said Miss Dunn. Gareth climbed down the ladder, sweating, careful not to look at Miss Dunn. Tall leylandii hedges surrounded three sides of the orphanage. She had given Gareth and Ross a week to finish pruning them, something that normally took a month. Gareth was to cut, Ross to pick up the clippings. Ross stepped back to get out of Dunn's sight. There was no point in both of them getting in trouble. As it was, only one side was finished.

"Mr Leonard tells me you've been lazy," said Miss Dunn.

Gareth kept his eyes downcast. He held the rusted shears in both hands. Their dented hickory handles were warm.

"Answer, boy!" said Miss Dunn.

"I've not been lazy," said Gareth.

"Mr Leonard doesn't lie." She stepped closer, the top of her head reaching his chin.

Gareth shook his head, and she slapped his face.

"No, Miss Dunn," he said.

She turned to Ross. "You'd have finished in a week, Ivan?"

Ross nodded.

"Detention," she said and left.

Ross smiled. "Mr Leonard's goin' to get you!"

Gareth automatically looked around. The mannequin was leaning against the side of the house, watching. Gareth climbed back up the ladder and continued working.

◆

Josey had seen everything from the scullery. She was scrubbing more bed sheets in the dolly tub. She had seen Miss Dunn talk to Gareth and heard what Ross had said. The miserably thin casement window was left permanently open so the laundry would dry.

She leaned in over the tub and craned her neck to see what Gareth had been looking at. There was Mr Leonard, watching the boys.

"Slut," said Noreen behind her. "I'll tell Miss Dunn you're lazy."

A gust of wind shook Mr Leonard. He swung around to look at her.

Noreen was folding the finished bed-linen. It never dried completely in the cramped space, but the sheets were no more than damp and therefore lighter than the heavy fresh washing, so it should have been the task of the smaller girls, Siobhan and Teal. But Noreen was allowed to do what she liked. She even got to lick the spoon Miss Dunn used for her jam. As it was, after Josey had washed the laundry, she had to help the two small girls wind the black winch to lower the heavy washing lines which criss-crossed the room, hang the sheets, and then wind them back up again to make sure there was enough room to continue washing. Even when lowered, the lines were higher than the girls' heads. Josey unrolled another ball of piss-stained laundry and dumped the sheet into the tub, forcing it down into the soap-slimy water with both hands, imagining it was Noreen.

◆

"Godfrey reappeared in the White Parlour with dry feet, and, since the truth must be told, with a sense of relief…" Josey was reading to the children. She had four of the smallest children on her bed with her. Gareth sat on the windowsill, the back of his hand against the cold, warped glass of the closed leaf. The other side was open to air the room. Lee lay on his bed.

A door slammed. Josey put the book down and the children scurried for the protection of their worn bedclothes. Miss Dunn came in and snapped off the light.

"Ivan!"

Gareth followed her out. Lee's eyes adjusted to the dark slowly. There was the sound of running water and eventually Gareth came back. Lee must have slept because when he looked again, Mr Leonard was in the doorway, his suit expanding and contracting as he breathed in the scent of the children.

◆

The rain sputtered over the garden. Gareth continued to work on the hedge. Lee had been given Ross's job, sweeping up the cuttings. It suited him fine as it meant he didn't have to worry about Ross, who was re-painting the blackboard in the unused second classroom. Lee and Gareth were wet through, their skin glowing white under their sodden shirts. Gareth almost slipped when he climbed down the ladder to reposition it. Lee held it steady.

"Is detention really that bad?" said Lee.

Gareth hadn't spoken since he'd come back from it.

"Josey said there was no detention here for a long time. It's my fault," said Lee.

When Gareth climbed back down the ladder, he sat on the lowest step, the shears in his lap.

"There used to be detention all the time when I arrived. Younger than you. It stopped because they all ran away: Arthur, Pat, Will, Sophie... I don't remember all of them."

"It's my fault," said Lee. "But my name is all I..." He stared over Gareth's back. Gareth wiped the rain off the blades of the shears with his hand and climbed the ladder again. Mr Leonard watched them from the attic, half out the window with his rubber hands on the dull roof slates. His brown woollen suit a glossy crow black in the rain.

❖

"Finished," said Gareth. The shears and the ladder were to go back under the stairs, but they glistened with rain. Putting them back wet would get him punished for carelessness. There was no sign of Mr Leonard, which meant he could be anywhere.

"Wait here." Gareth ran to the woodpile at the back of the orphanage, near the Sick Room, and hid them behind the unused firewood. They were rusty, so even if he could find an old rag to dry them, he would still get in trouble for making it dirty.

There was some food in the kitchen when they went in. Josey had left one of the clean bed sheets there for them to dry themselves off with, as there were no towels at the Lambs of Our Lord. She was still washing in the scullery with Siobhan, who was wetting the bed almost every night. Josey had promised to read more of Silas Marner if there was time before Miss Dunn switched the light off. Siobhan started humming as she hung the sheets up with Josey.

Siobhan went to pull another one out of the dolly tub. Mr Leonard was at the window, staring in. She screamed. Josey turned at the noise. Her heart raced, but she pretended to ignore Mr Leonard, and pulled at the sheet, calling roughly to Siobhan to help. She kept talking until they were back at the clothesline. There was a wet patch where Siobhan was standing and the bitter ammonia tang of urine.

❖

Ross was waiting for Lee in the bathroom again when they went upstairs. The blackboard paint was thick and oil-based, the fumes clung to the children, giving them headaches. Ross had checked that Gareth was already asleep, and as soon as the others had left the washroom, Enda blocked the door. Ross grabbed Lee in a headlock. When Lee was half-choked, Ross pushed him to the ground, then stood with one foot on his neck.

"Lick it, Ivan," he said, holding the metre-stick to Lee's face. Lee continued to struggle, and Ross pushed down on his windpipe.

"Come on, Ivan. You're in detention now. I'm Mr Leonard, lick my stick," he said.

Lee struggled to move Ross's foot. His face was red. Slowly, he dropped his hands and stopped struggling.

"Shit!" Ross and Enda ran into the hallway.

"Where are you going?" said Miss Dunn.

"Bed, Miss Dunn," said Ross, who stopped running, but couldn't keep his leg from jiggling. A cough came from the washroom, followed by wheezing gasps. Miss Dunn nodded. "No running," she said.

"Thank you, Miss Dunn," said Ross.

She entered the washroom, where Lee was making his way to the door. "You've left the tap running, Ivan." She slammed his hand onto the metal tap and crushed his fingers as she closed the tap with it. He started crying. "If you're not in bed, you must have too much energy, Ivan." She dragged him out to the stairs. "Start running. Down and back." She turned. Mr Leonard was watching from her apartment. "Thank you, Mr Leonard, I have everything under control here." After a pause: "Mr Leonard, I have everything in control." Lee had arrived back at the top of the stairs and turned to go back down. "Go to bed, Ivan," she said.

Six

GARETH WAS STILL BEING PUNISHED with detention. Lee didn't want to know what happened there, but he remembered Ross's promise to leave him alone if he was only brave enough to look. He couldn't sleep anyway, with the pain in his hand and around his neck. The soft breathing around him told him that the others were already asleep. When he heard running water from Miss Dunn's apartment, he snuck out of the bedroom.

◆

Bitter perfume blew from under the door. Lee had tried the keyhole, but it had been stuffed with swirls of petrified paper. Now he lay on the ground and looked through the gap between the door and the threshold. The room held a mint green club chair with royal pink roses, a long rosewood table under the window which held books and a jam jar. A standing lamp with a light brown cord lampshade stood behind the club chair. Mr Leonard stood on the other side of the chair. Miss Dunn sat in it. Gareth knelt before her. He was naked. A fire blazed in the fireplace and a breeze blew under

the door, dried Lee's eyes so that he had to keep blinking.

Miss Dunn wore Mr Leonard's suit and boots and held the metre-stick in one hand. From under the door Lee could see Mr Leonard's bare torso, which was split across the abdomen, with "SIEGEL" in large letters, across the bottom half. There was a cavity in the top half, where his heart should have been. But his wooden body was a healthy tan, while Gareth's skin blazed white.

Gareth was bent over on all fours, tapping at the ground. No. He held a dustpan and brush. He crawled around the chair, sweeping at the floorboards. He wasn't completely naked, he had a black belt around his waist. His knees and elbows, hips and buttocks pushed out painfully from under his skin. He disappeared behind the chair and reappeared from behind Mr Leonard, facing the door. Lee found it hard to breathe. He was somehow more scared that Gareth would see him than that Mr Leonard would. From this angle, Lee could see it wasn't a belt. It was the strap of a small apron to cover his genitals.

Gareth looked towards the door and Lee started back. The door tapped against the frame; Lee had been leaning against it to see into the room. His stomach churned. Had they heard?

"Ivan!"

Lee held his breath, but Miss Dunn was calling Gareth. He crawled on his knees until he was in front of her again.

Miss Dunn conferred with the naked Mr Leonard.

"Mr Leonard says you're still lazy. How much dirt have you collected?"

Gareth held out the dustpan. It didn't look like there was anything on it. Hadn't Noreen cleaned up earlier today?

"Don't look at me, you filthy animal!" Miss Dunn slapped his face.

Gareth averted his face and held out the dustpan.

She tutted. "Again!" Gareth crawled around the chair again, this time with Miss Dunn following him, whipping his bare backside.

"You missed some," said Miss Dunn. He turned around. She stood right behind him. Tall in Mr Leonard's boots.

"Show me," she said. He stood, holding out the dustpan with his eyes averted. The apron was pushed out in front of him. Lee wanted to leave but was terrified that if he moved, the door would bang again and all three of them would catch him and make him play the game. His face was burning with shame. The breeze from under the door felt cool in comparison.

Miss Dunn had her back to the door, pushing himself against Gareth. Herself, it was just that she was wearing Mr Leonard's clothes. Mr Leonard stared at the door. He knew Lee was there. He was waiting for him to make a sound to spring forward and grab him, drag him into detention.

Lee wished he'd stayed in bed. He didn't want to see any more. But if he looked away, Mr Leonard could sneak up on him. He had to keep watching to stay safe. So he saw Miss Dunn wrench Gareth's apron off. "What are you hiding?" she said. "How dare you bring this filthy little thing into my apartment!" She slapped it, and Gareth winced.

She gestured to the jar on the rosewood table. "Get rid of it," she said.

◆

A hand grabbed Lee's shoulder.

"What are you doing?" said Josey.

This was the chance he had been waiting for. Josey would take him back to the dormitory. But her voice was loud in the empty hallway; they must have heard her. He looked back under the door to see if they'd been caught. He couldn't see anything. There was something in the way.

Mr Leonard's smooth wooden head was lying in front of him, behind the door. Lee scrambled backwards and ran with Josey to the dormitory. As they reached it, they heard Dunn's apartment door open, followed by the stamp of Mr Leonard's boots on the floorboards.

Lee made to get into bed, but Josey stopped him. "Get undressed!" she said. Around them, the children were woken by the approaching steps. Josey had her cardigan on over her pyjamas. In her panic the top button had become snarled up in a loose thread around the buttonhole. Lee came back to help her, tugged and the button span off. The door opened and without thinking they both sprang into her bed. She pulled the bedclothes up high, lying on her side to hide Lee behind her, despite knowing they would be found. Miss Leonard came in. She wore a long nightgown that covered her, everything except for Mr Leonard's boots. She stopped in the doorway.

Seven

"THERE WAS A CHILD," she said, and started pacing the room. "A disgusting, insignificant creature. Thin and pale and dirty, always dirty. But worse than the dirt was what the child was like inside. Because it was never satisfied. Even its parents were sick of it, always asking questions and never believing the answers. So they sent it to a school far away." The rustling of scratchy bedclothes had stopped. No one wanted to draw attention to themselves. "The teacher there was a wise and beautiful woman who knew all about tiresome children. But even she lost her patience. She'd tell it to sit during class and it would ask why it couldn't stand. When it was dinnertime, the child wanted to know why it couldn't have what it used to eat. At bedtime it wanted to know why it had to lie down if it wasn't tired. And the teacher would explain and the child would still cry out 'but why?'

"So one day she decided to teach it why. She put biscuits in a metal tin with laughing people printed around the sides. She had told the filthy child to do its homework, so naturally it had asked why and was

staring out the window instead. While it wasn't looking, she put two hungry rats in the tin as well. She told the child that if it went to bed straight away, without asking any questions, it could have the biscuits for breakfast. 'Why can't I have them now?' it asked. She told it she had put rats in the tin. 'Why?' it asked. So she sent it off to bed and told it there would be no biscuits for breakfast, after all. In the middle of the night the child, which often crawled around poking its nose into everybody's business, got up and went to the tin. And when it opened the tin, the rats jumped out and—having already eaten the biscuits and finding them not to their liking—they jumped straight for the child's eyes, eating them up and burrowing into its brain until it was dead.

"And in the morning the teacher saw the dead body and said, 'That's why.'"

Lee heard someone crying.

"Anna," said Miss Dunn, standing at the bed closest to the door. Noreen stood up, shivering.

Miss Dunn moved on. "Anna." Siobhan climbed quickly out of her bed. Miss Dunn sniffed at her sheets before she moved to the next bed.

There was a commotion at the door. Noreen had remained beside her bed, and Gareth had stumbled into her when he came in. She screamed and tried to push him away, both of them falling over in the dark. In the disruption, Josey elbowed Lee. He rolled out of her bed and across the floor to his own, sliding under the sheets as Miss Dunn pulled Gareth off Noreen.

"It was an accident," he said. "Sorry, Miss Dunn." She left them standing where they were for the rest of the night.

◆

The beatings were getting worse. Josey could barely stand to look at him. Lee had lost two teeth, one of his eyes was swollen shut, his lips were lacerated and his windpipe rattled when he spoke. All because he wouldn't answer when she called him. Though he hadn't told Ross what he had seen during detention, the boys were leaving him alone for now. Miss Dunn had also prescribed a diet of water, three times a day, no solids. Josey smuggled food to him, which he ate while the others washed before bed.

"'Insubordination,' Ivan!" Dunn cracked the metre-stick across the top of Lee's skull. Gareth stood up and headed for the board.

"No!" said Miss Dunn.

"I thought you called me, Miss Dunn," he said.

"No!" she said. "I called Ivan."

"Yes, Miss Dunn."

"This one! This arrogant brat! Ivan!" Tears ran from Lee's eyes, snot from his nose.

"Miss Dunn!" said Josey. "I know the answer, Miss Dunn. Please, Miss!"

Dunn gave Josey a look, then smiled and bent to whisper into Lee's ear. There was a creak as Mr Leonard leaned in from his corner to hear what she said. Miss Dunn straightened and started to call again, "Iv—" but Lee was already walking to the board. Eleven of the twelve words were already done, the last saved for him:

Crow;

Duty;

Pride;

Shame;

Wash;

Sin;

Sloth;

Wicked;

Obey;

Bad;

Dirty.

Lee scrawled I N S U B O R D I N A T I O N below them.

"At last!" said Miss Dunn. "He finally decides to do what he's told. Sit, Lee! Well, was that so hard?"

A murmur ran through the classroom. Dunn's lips twisted in anger. He had tricked her. Insubordination. She walked behind Lee back to his desk and as he sat she slashed at his face with her fingernails, tearing the skin and knocking him over. Blood trickled from Lee's ear.

Eight

"I'M RUNNING AWAY," said Lee. His voice was a croak.

Josey slapped him. "I'm sorry," she said. Lee and Gareth stared at her. "I shouldn't have done that. But don't let anyone hear you. You can't." They were in the kitchen, cleaning the cooker and the floor again, the last ones still up.

"People have. Arthur, Sophie..." Lee stopped.

"I should have gone with Sophie," said Josey. "Dunn hated her. She had beautiful hair. She left without me."

"Come with us," said Lee. "We can wait until it's dark and then run for it. Find out where Sophie and the others went. Join them. They must be somewhere better than this."

"Dunn will kill us!" said Josey.

"She's doing that anyway," said Gareth. "Come with us."

"What about the rest?"

"We can come back for them with the police."

Lee went to the scullery to empty out the bucket of dirty mop water.

"What is detention like?" said Josey.

Gareth looked away. "I have to get out of here."

Josey touched him on the arm, ignoring the shudder that went through him at the unexpected touch.

"I have a plan," said Lee as he returned.

Miss Dunn appeared in the doorway and they went upstairs. She followed them until they passed Mr Leonard's dim shape in the hallway. As the children climbed the stairs, she stopped and Lee looked down to see Mr Leonard listening intently to what she was telling him.

Miss Dunn no longer just picked on Lee anymore. Her eyes constantly scanned the classroom for trouble. She would call Lee, then Siobhan, then the other children at random until only Gareth was left. While the others were lashed with the stick or dragged by their hair or bent over her desk to be whipped on their bare backsides, Gareth was always punished with more detention. The lessons themselves became increasingly vague. Dunn stared out the window between bursts of anger.

It was Mr Leonard's fault. Though they were all scared of him, he had kept Miss Dunn under control. Now he sometimes watched over them while they slept but left control of the classroom to Miss Dunn, who, apart from the bed-wetters, left the children mostly alone outside it. Any girl who wet herself was made to squat for hours in a bucket of cold water while she scrubbed the boys with an old scouring pad. Anyone who cried was sent to the Sick Room until they were better. But, of course, Mr Leonard couldn't come out of the apartment during the day anymore, because Miss Dunn had stolen his clothes and was wearing them herself.

Mr Leonard stood over Josey's bed when Lee woke. The room was silent. There was only the sound of breathing from Mr Leonard and the ticking of the tree's branches on the window. Mr Leonard's rubber hand reached for Josey's neck. She gasped at the touch and Lee jumped out of bed. He barrelled into the figure, wrapping his arms around its waist. Mr Leonard buckled and tried to twist away. Lee fell onto the mannequin and beat at its face.

Mr Leonard struggled under him. Gareth had joined him and was kicking the dummy in the head with his bare feet. Mr Leonard groaned as more children arrived. Siobhan pulled at its hair, Noreen stamped on its legs, but it rose, shrugging off the blows. They backed away and Mr Leonard smoothed a hand over his face, wiping off blood. Miss Dunn. She stared around her.

"Ivan! Anna! Get to bed instantly!" The children fled.

"Come, Mr Leonard," she called over her shoulder and left.

Nine

VISITORS WERE EXPECTED. Mr Leonard waited in the attic. Miss Dunn at the front door. Lee was out of sight in the Sick Room, separate from the main building.

It was a wide shed with an asbestos sheet roof, also used to store broken machinery and furniture. There was one grimy window, which let in a little light and it stank sweetly of machine oil, petrol and decaying matter. The floor was packed earth, hard around the walls, softer in the middle as if recently turned. Lee sat on a pile of jute fertiliser sacks close to the door, where the air was fresher. In the dark, he listened for the sound of the car engine, though he didn't know who would be coming and why they should want to look for him.

The children were in the garden. They had been warned to wash with particular care. A skipping rope, wooden bats and rubber balls had been dispensed from a tan leather suitcase. Everything smelt of camphor. It was hard not to get excited, but no one had ever been adopted from the Lambs of Our Lord orphanage.

Miss Dunn marched to the gate when she heard the engine. "Mr and Mrs Colton?" she said, after a fern green Ford saloon pulled up outside.

They nodded, and she unlocked the gate with a key from the leather strap around her neck. Mrs Colton smiled at the children. They stared back.

"Let me take you to the office." Miss Dunn swept the Coltons towards the building. "Mr Leonard is watching, children," she said.

Gareth and Josey hurried towards the Sick Room as the front door closed. Gareth fished out the garden shears from where he had hidden them behind the wood pile. He inserted one of the blades into the loop of the padlock and twisted. The padlock was thick, but the wood of the door was rotten. Soon there was enough of a gap between the hasp and the door and he slipped the shears in, wrenching the lock off the door in a quick movement. When the door opened, Lee saw Mr Leonard watching them from the attic. But if they hurried, he'd never get down the stairs in time to stop them. Lee ran to the scullery, where he was able to squeeze through the open casement window. Gareth hammered the lock back onto the door, and then he and Josey waited for Lee to let them in through the back door. They headed for the office.

They slammed into the room, interrupting Miss Dunn.

"... requirements. Unfortunately, most children here are unsuitable for... " she rose.

"Please," Josey went straight to Mrs Colton. "Help us! Miss Dunn did this." She pushed Lee towards them. The Coltons recoiled from his eye, which was swollen shut, and from his face camouflaged with bruises ranging from yellow to fresh, vivid purple. From the smell of the Sick Room that had seeped into his clothes.

"Josephine, what are you doing with Lee?" said Miss Dunn. She turned to the visitors, inserted herself between them and the children. "This is little Lee," she said. "He's only just arrived. Thank God. He's safe now."

"Please!" said Josey as Miss Dunn pushed her to the door.

Colour rose in Miss Dunn's cheeks. "Gareth, see Josephine does as she's told."

"Please," Josey continued to address the Coltons. "Miss Dunn is crazy. Look at Lee. Mr Leonard comes into our room at night. Gareth! Tell them what he does to you at detention."

Mrs Colton was a plump, pretty woman in her thirties. Her eyes crinkled with concern as she looked at Gareth. Mr Colton looked quiet and confident. Both of them looked clean and nice and innocent. Miss Dunn turned to Gareth. "Well then. Tell us all your little story, Gareth. Let's get this over with."

Gareth blushed. The words weren't there to explain it. If he told them, Dunn would deny it and he'd have to tell the story again and again, in front of pretty Mrs Colton. He looked away.

"SHE," said Lee, pointing to Miss Dunn, "strips Mr Leonard and makes Gareth—"

"That's enough," said Miss Dunn. "How dare you talk like that about Mr Leonard!" She dragged Lee and Josey upstairs and locked them into one of the unused rooms.

The Coltons were whispering heatedly when she returned.

"Let me apologise for Josephine," said Miss Dunn. "She means well, I'm sure."

"It must be tough," said Mr Colton. "Just yourself and Mr Leonard, I understand?"

"Correct. The children help with housework but there simply isn't enough money for outside—"

"Perhaps," said Mr Colton, "It's nonsense, of course, but it might help the children calm down if they knew someone was listening to them?"

"I don't think—"

"I insist," said Mr Colton, looking at his wife for encouragement. She nodded. "Perhaps Mr Leonard could show us?"

Miss Dunn pulled herself up and stared. Mr Colton waited.

"Mr Leonard is not here."

"In the garden, you told the children he was watching."

She sighed. "I'm alone. I didn't want them to know. They act up if they think they can get away with it."

"We don't want to cause a fuss," said Mrs Colton. "Perhaps we could just speak to the children again?"

"Of course. Not Josephine, you'll only encourage her. I'll get Noreen, and you can ask anything you like." Miss Dunn opened the office door. Mr Leonard toppled into the room.

Ten

MRS COLTON SCREAMED.

"Mr Leonard!" said Miss Dunn. She licked her lips and turned to the Coltons. "Can you believe it? That's what they call the dummy. Oh, I knew they must be up to something!" She picked the mannequin up and stood it against the wall. "They usually wait until I am alone. I'll walk around a corner and find him waiting for me."

She ushered them out of the office. "Well, come along!"

"That doll is awful!" said Mrs Colton.

"And to call it Mr Leonard just seems so disrespectful. But don't leave with the wrong impression. I assure you they behave themselves most of the time. They just need to let a little of the devil out, now and again."

"But where did it come from? And what's wrong with the head?" A yell from the garden interrupted her.

"Oh, he's always been like that," she said.

"Aren't you going to see what's wrong?" said Mr Colton.

"Of course. As soon as we've spoken to Noreen."

The yelling got louder.

"It sounds serious."

"They get fractious when left alone. That's all." Miss Dunn opened the front door. "There's always a victim, isn't there?"

Outside, Siobhan was on the ground, Noreen stood over her, brandishing the skipping rope. Miss Dunn strode between them and pulled Noreen away. Siobhan lay on the ground, crying.

The Coltons looked at each other.

"Look, we'll leave you to it, Miss Dunn."

"Are you sure? Noreen is right here."

"Really. Thank you for your time."

In the car, Mrs Colton shivered. "That poor woman. I could have sworn the dummy jumped at me!"

◆

Miss Dunn lined the children up against the back wall of the house with a view of the Sick Room once the Coltons had left. "Your behaviour was appalling today. You let me down and you let the orphanage down. Who knows what impression those people will have of me?"

The sky darkened, and Miss Dunn went inside. Out of the corner of her eye, Josey saw Mr Leonard behind the scullery window. The cold and damp crept into their legs from the ground. Teal fell, and Miss Dunn came out and made her take off her shoes to stand barefoot in the wet grass as punishment. They weren't allowed back in before classes the next day, and then had to remain standing at their desks, shivering and sniffing. Siobhan leant heavily against Josey, her legs shaking, but she managed to stay standing. There was no food and when they went to bed, all the blankets had been removed.

"Get undressed for bed," said Miss Dunn. "If anyone is cold, they can blame Ivan, Ivan and Anna."

Sleep was impossible. They coughed and shivered through the night. The dormitory window remained open, despite the unseasonably cold April weather. The next day was worse. Every cough was punished with six lashes of the metre-stick. The girls across one hand, the boys across both hands. Josey's head felt waterlogged, and it was hard to stay awake despite the ache in her ribs from coughing through the night. Worse was the tickle of a cough creeping up her throat with every exhalation.

Gareth shook as he stifled a cough. He was sweating in the frigid air. He had returned with his hair still wet from detention to the chilled dormitory. Miss Dunn paced between them.

Noreen coughed, loud and hacking beside Josey.

"Anna," said Miss Dunn. Josey waited for Noreen to rise. Noreen turned and stared at Josey.

"Anna!"

Josey turned. "Miss, I—"

"Up!" The metre-stick crashed onto the desk, pressing another welt into the thick varnish on the red-brown wood. Josey stood. The cough was right behind her teeth. She bit back on it.

"Hand."

Josey lifted her hand, palm out. It was the first time she'd been punished. "But—" She coughed. Dunn lashed at her fingers, the meat of her palm. Twelve blows. Her hand burned and ached. Miss Dunn moved away, a line of sweat at her hairline, her breath heavy. Josey crumpled into her seat. Noreen coughed again. A single loud bark to call Miss Dunn back.

Eleven

GARETH SWEPT THE PATHWAY around the outside of the house in the rain. Josey was in the scullery. They were talking through the open window. There were so many bedclothes wet with urine and fever sweat that they had to be done before class started.

"The keys are always around her neck. We can't get them," said Gareth.

"When she's asleep?" said Josey, scrubbing a bed sheet

"No. And not when she's in the bath. But she locks the doors, we can't get into her room, anyway."

"When she's in the..." Josey trailed off. "OK, so she doesn't always have them around her neck."

"It doesn't matter, we can't get them!" Gareth coughed. His whole body shook. His eyes were hollow. Only his grip on the brush kept him standing.

"We have to."

"We can," said Lee from the doorway. Josey jumped.

"Lee!"

"Where are the keys when she's in the bath?"

"She puts them on a chair in the bathroom. She puts them with her clothes."

"When does she have a bath?" asked Lee.

Gareth couldn't look at them. He hunched over into himself when he spoke. "During detention. Tonight."

"We can definitely get out if we have the keys?"

"It opens all the doors. It's just a couple of miles to the town. We can hide in the hedges if she comes after us. Go to the police."

"Then be ready," said Lee.

Thick clouds decorated the sky, and Miss Dunn spent most of the class staring out at them. When she did speak, she addressed Mr Leonard, although he was still upstairs in the apartment. Once the children were in bed and Gareth had been collected for detention, Josey pulled on a second pair of socks and an extra jumper, which she'd left hidden in the scullery after it was dry. Once she was dressed, she lay back under the bedclothes to wait in case Miss Dunn came prowling around.

Her heart beat painfully against her ribcage. They'd forgotten about Mr Leonard.

Twelve

MISS DUNN'S APARTMENT lay at the back of the house. It consisted of a sitting room, which opened off the hallway. Her bedroom opened off that to the right. There were two doors on the left. One led into a kitchenette, the other into a narrow bathroom. Miss Dunn sat in the armchair in the sitting room with the light off, felt herself fading into the dark as night fell early. She waited until the sounds of the children's scuffling feet, the banging washroom door faded away, and detention could wait no longer. She left, Mr Leonard's boots clacking on the floorboards.

Lee waited in one of the toilet cubicles. As soon as the boots passed by, he ran for the door. The toilets were in the corner furthest from the door: she could already be coming back by the time he reached the hall. He spent several seconds alone in the corridor, expecting to be caught as he pulled the washroom door quietly closed. He ran for her apartment, keeping close to the walls: the floorboards squeaked less there. The door was closed. He tested the handle. It opened, and he darted in. As he closed it behind him, he heard her

voice. "Ivan!" He had to hope she was calling Gareth. He took a deep breath and looked around for somewhere to hide. The bathroom would be best. That was where the keys would be. There was no cover there. In the sitting room, there was only the table. He could only hide under it if she didn't put the light on. And he didn't want to be there if she was going to make Gareth be naked again. Footsteps approached, and he crawled under her bed, hoping he hadn't trapped himself.

Miss Dunn turned on the lamp in the sitting room. Gareth was behind her. He was a head taller but looked too skinny. The shadows around his eyes were accentuated by the low light and his forehead shone.

"Get undressed," she said. "Run the bath." She went into the bedroom. Gareth's chilblained feet disappeared into the bathroom. Water started to run, the noise making Lee's stomach feel funny. The sound of detention.

"You're filthy," said Miss Dunn. "I think you court detention on purpose." Clothing rustled, and the bed creaked as she sat to tug off her boots. "Do you?"

"No, Miss Dunn."

"I think you do." Her voice was hard.

"Yes, Miss Dunn."

"Stand at the window until I'm ready," she said. "Do you think I enjoy having to do this?"

"No, Miss Dunn,"

"I know what boys are like. Someone has to keep the girls safe from you." The bed creaked again as Miss Dunn stood. From the position of his feet, Gareth must still be looking out the window.

"What do you say, Ivan?"

"Thank you, Miss Dunn."

"Go to the bathroom."

They disappeared and water splashed.

"You've been looking at me," she said.

"No, Miss Dunn."

"This doesn't lie."

Water splashed for a while. Lee's neck ached as he stared towards the bathroom. When they came out, they got dressed. Miss Dunn put on Mr Leonard's clothes, and Gareth wore her dress and stockings. She sat in the chair in the living room and made Gareth kneel in front of her as she ate jam straight from the jar. When she was finished, she grabbed him by the hair and pulled him to bed.

Lee waited as long as he could. When he heard deep breathing, he crawled out from under the bed. Resisting the urge to look behind him, he crawled all the way to the bathroom in the dark.

The keys were on the chair. He put one hand on top of the bunch and slid the other underneath, holding them so they couldn't clink together. He stayed low as he moved to the apartment door. The first key rasped in the lock, but wouldn't turn. The next one went half in and stuck. His hands were wet with sweat and he couldn't grip it properly to pull it back out. Another tug and it was free. The keys clicked as he swayed backwards. Bed sheets rustled. He waited. Adrenaline flooded his body, and his hands shook as he tried the next key. It turned. He could feel the weight of the lock shift. A click and the bolt slid back into the door.

He tip-toed into the bedroom. Gareth's eyes were open. He was wrapped in Miss Dunn's arms. He shook his head as Lee approached. Miss Dunn breathed heavily, but Gareth was entangled in her grasp. Lee grabbed a cushion from the chair and returned. Gareth rolled away from Miss Dunn, centimetre by slow centimetre. Lee leaned in over both of them and pushed the cushion into the gap that appeared. Lee found the sound of her breathing hypnotic. It grew louder and louder. He didn't think he was breathing himself, didn't think Gareth was either. His arms ached from craning over the bed.

When the cushion was in place, Gareth rolled the rest of the way out of bed and they crawled to the door. Lee pulled Gareth's arm to slow him down. In his panic, he was too fast, too loud. They stopped.

Mr Leonard was sitting in the chair, his rubber hands dangling over the armrests.

Thirteen

THEY WAITED, the silence of the teacher's apartment rushing in their ears, then Gareth moved to the bathroom to get his clothes. The mannequin remained motionless while Lee waited, but he could still hear the deep breathing and couldn't tell whether it came from the bedroom behind him, or the sitting room. He moved to the unlocked door, his scalp creeping, and turned the handle slowly, wondering if Mr Leonard's hands would feel cold or warm when they grabbed him. He heard the sound of movement, and he looked back. Gareth. In trousers and unbuttoned shirt.

Lee opened the door. The hallway was clear, the teachers both behind them. There was a tiny sticky noise as the door opened, pulling away from the thick paint in the frame. A floorboard creaked behind them. The heavy breathing had stopped. Gareth dashed to the dormitory. Lee slammed the door closed behind them and locked it. It shook in its frame as it was pounded from the other side. He ran. Gareth was waiting with Josey outside the dormitory, their eyes wide. They ran down the stairs together.

The first key he tried opened the front door of the orphanage. They ran for the gate, which had a large lock, so Lee fumbled through the bunch for the largest key.

"Come on!" said Josey.

"I locked them in," said Lee.

Before he could try the first key, the garden lit up. The upstairs hall light had come on. It shone through the landing window, picking out the three of them in the dark garden.

"No!"

The lock was old and stiff, and none of the keys wanted to turn. Gareth grabbed the keys from Lee and tried again as Mr Leonard appeared, loping across the lawn towards them.

"He's coming!" said Josey. She kept her eyes on the dummy. He looked so strange without his clothes, his torso in two halves, his joints jerky. He had almost reached them, and she screamed as he stretched out a hand. They ran for the hedge, leaving the keys stuck in the gate. He grabbed the keys and held one up. The one they should have used. He turned towards the house. Another Mr Leonard had appeared in the landing window, struggling with Siobhan. Miss Dunn. Still in Mr Leonard's clothes. She picked up the small girl, ready to throw her down the steps.

"No!" Josey ran to the house. The others followed. When they were in the hallway below her, Miss Dunn put Siobhan down. Then shoved her. She tumbled down the stairs, coming to a stop in front of them. Miss Dunn stalked down to them. All the blood had left her face.

She unbuckled Mr Leonard's belt. "Hands!" she said, her voice shaking.

Siobhan lay sobbing on the floor. The others put their hands out for their punishment. Instead of lashing them Miss Dunn looped the belt around their wrists and tightened it. She grabbed Siobhan with her other hand and dragged them out the open door towards the Sick Room. Siobhan screamed as her leg was bent and again as it thumped down the steps.

Mr Leonard still stood at the gate, watching Miss Dunn. She opened the padlock with her spare set of keys and locked the children into the ripe, faecal-smelling dark.

"It's broken," said Josey. Siobhan hung to her, crying. The Sick Room was pitch black. They sat near the door. Lee felt for the fertiliser bags.

"We can wrap it round her leg," he said.

Siobhan screamed when Josey pulled it tight. "It'll hurt less later," she said.

The night was cold and Gareth pushed some of the bags under the door to stop the draught. They wrapped themselves in the rest. The sweet iron stink of rot and oil pressed in on them. Despite the pain, Siobhan fell asleep in Josey's arms. Lee sat with his arms wrapped around his legs. Gareth got up and prowled around the shed. His stomach knotted painfully. There was the dread at what Miss Dunn might do to them and the burning humiliation of having been seen during detention. There was nothing useful in the shed. They could smash a window with some of the furniture, but that would only draw attention to themselves and they would still be stuck in the garden. There was a spade with a snapped handle, but he didn't know how effective it would be against Mr Leonard. The blade was thin and rusted, brittle. When he noticed the softer earth in the centre of the shed, he scrabbled at it. Perhaps they could dig their way out. It was icy cold and loose. He picked up the spade.

The smell in the Sick Room grew worse, and Siobhan woke as it tickled her throat. He could barely see the earth he lifted, but could feel its weight. He was making good progress, already knee deep in the hole. Then the spade wouldn't go in any further, catching on something. Something wrapped in crusted cloth. He pulled at it and fell backwards. Lee disentangled himself from the bags and went to look. Then had to touch it to identify it in the dark. It was an arm. He scrabbled at the dirt, unearthed another one.

"What is it?" said Josey.

"Don't come over," said Gareth.

There were six small bodies.

"Stay here," said Josey to Siobhan, and made her way over to the hole.

The moon came out from behind the clouds and lit up blonde curls.

"Sophie!"

Fourteen

MISS DUNN tried on her old clothes. Her apartment was strewn with polyester, wool and leather. The children made her feel hard and sour. She wanted to feel soft. Like a mother. But they weren't her children. In the mirror she only saw the fat settling on her jaws and elbows, on her belly, the extra folds on her thighs. Her hair was thin, too. Exhausted. They were using her up, sucking her dry. If she gave them a chance, they'd finish her off. None of her clothes looked good on her anymore. She needed to be hard, not like the doughy jowls that made her lips look thinner than they were. Mr Leonard took his clothes off again and handed them to her. She put them on. Better. His baggy trousers covered up the fat, the greying flesh. She was taller in his boots. They wouldn't mess with her if she was tall. Better. Her hair was stringy, it didn't suit her. She tied it back. Better. Only her face let her down, bags under her eyes, a few hairs sprouting along her jawline and nose. She opened a fresh pair of tights and pulled them over her head. The nylon held her skin firmly, made her smooth. But it wasn't better. She pulled the tights off and drew two eyebrows on them with mascara. Put them back on. Better.

She picked up her metre-stick and walked to the Sick Room. The grass swallowed her footsteps; the blades crunching lushly underfoot. There was no sound from the Sick Room. The night was peaceful. Then she heard whispering through the wooden door. She raised her rubber hand with the metre-stick. It was Mr Leonard who knocked on the door. The whispering stopped. He unlocked the door with the key around his neck. He wished he didn't have to sort out these messes for Miss Dunn. She was getting scared of the children as they grew older, bigger. She wouldn't get away with this forever. That's why she needed him. There was nothing they could do to him.

He stepped into the shed towards the sound, and Gareth dived out of the shadows at him.

"Go!" he said, tumbling Mr Leonard to the ground. Josey and Lee carried Siobhan out. Gareth grabbed the metre-stick.

Miss Dunn's head hurt. When she started to rise, Gareth slashed the metre-stick across her face. But Mr Leonard didn't feel pain and continued to rise. Gareth ran. Mr Leonard took a breath through the tear in his tights and followed.

Lee pushed at the front door. It was closed, they were locked out. Mr Leonard stalked into view around the corner behind them, and they continued running, holding Siobhan up as best they could.

"She can't run," said Gareth.

"We can't leave her," said Josey.

"You keep going," said Gareth. "Get the others, and I'll hide with her. We'll be okay." They had run all the way around the orphanage by now, and he ducked behind the Sick Room with Siobhan as Lee squeezed through the scullery window. Josey waited near the far corner until Mr Leonard—Dunn, it had to be Dunn, surely?—appeared behind her before continuing to run. "Go!" said Josey, pretending to talk to the others so Dunn would follow her.

Lee was waiting in the front hall to let Josey in, but without the key it wouldn't open from the inside, either.

"Hurry!" said Josey. Then Miss Dunn appeared, and she continued running. The figure loomed up at the door and Lee backed away. He went up the stairs. His heart felt too big for his chest, shaking him with each beat. He breathed through his open mouth, sweating at how loud it rushed in his ears. There were footsteps in the dormitory. Not the soft padding of the children, but the hard chip of wooden feet on floorboards. Mr Leonard. At the turn in the stairs, he looked away from the dormitory door. In the landing window he could only see his own reflection: a thin boy with a large head, wide eyes, cuts and bruises. He stayed close to the wall, listening for the sound of the key in the front door's lock. The wall soaked up the heat of his hand when he touched it. There was a light on in the teacher's apartment. He made it past the dormitory. Now both teachers were behind him. When he reached the apartment, he pulled the door closed and went to the window. Josey was still running, close to the back door, almost hidden behind the jutting roof of the scullery. He opened the window.

"Hey!" He pointed. Josey looked up. "The ladder!"

It was still lying at the woodpile. She was just about to pick it up, but jumped behind the pile instead. Miss Dunn was back. Lee leaned back out of view. She scanned the garden, continued walking, then decided to double back, apparently hoping the children would run straight into her. After a second, Josey emerged with the ladder. She dragged the ladder to the low roof of the scullery. She moved slowly, the ladder weighing her down. It rattled as she stood it up, leaned it against the wall, started climbing. Lee could almost grab her hand when Dunn came running for her. She had doubled back again. Either a trick or she had heard the noise. Josey climbed another step, slipping on the thin rungs, then jumped onto the sloping roof as Dunn reached for her. Almost more by accident, Josey's foot knocked the ladder away. She slid on the tiles and Lee grabbed her hand, holding on to the window frame with his free hand, the one that was cut and bruised and swollen. There was no way he could pull her up, but she stopped slipping, found a foothold, and was able to pull herself in through the window.

They had to get the children away before Dunn or Leonard hurt any more of them. They ran for the dormitory, where Mr Leonard was standing at the window, as if he had been watching what had been happening outside. He moved towards them in the dark.

"We're leaving" Josey shouted at him. "Everyone get up!" Josey and Lee grabbed at some of the younger children, who were sitting up in bed but too scared by the dummy to move. Mr Leonard kept coming. Josey pulled the children out of their beds to the door, and Lee blocked Mr Leonard by shoving the beds in his way.

"We found the other children" said Josey. "We're leaving." More of them joined her at the door, jumping across beds away from the dummy, and they pushed into the corridor. Mr Leonard watched them go.

Miss Dunn was at the bottom of the stairs. The leather strap with the keys swung around her neck. Mr Leonard clacked into the light on his wooden feet behind them. He was still naked. Something had been rolled up and squashed into the cavity in his chest. The children crowded together at the top of the stairs as the teachers advanced.

"Mr Leonard!" called Miss Dunn.

The sudden noise behind them was Gareth. He ran out of the teacher's apartment and tackled Mr Leonard. They crashed down the stairs. Gareth was on top as they came to a stop half-way down. Miss Dunn moved towards them. The leather strap swung forward and Lee ran for it. He slipped and barged into Miss Dunn, knocking them both into the front hall. There was a sharp pain in his side when he struggled to get up.

Fifteen

"NOW!" Josey pulled the smaller children down the stairs. Gareth stood over Mr Leonard until they were past. He helped Lee up and reached for the key strap, still around Dunn's neck. She started to move, and he tugged at it. Her head lifted and then thumped back on the floor. Lee was holding his side, unable to stand properly. They got the door open, and the children poured outside. Gareth had to call them as they scattered throughout the garden. The lock on the gate was stiff, and Dunn appeared in the doorway behind them while Lee was still trying to turn the key. Mr Leonard was behind her but moving more slowly, his leg bent oddly as they staggered towards the children. Lee let Josey try the key and ran at Miss Dunn. He swerved at the last minute, avoiding her grasping hands. He kept running, and she followed him around the side of the house. Mr Leonard stopped for a moment, looking from the children to Miss Dunn, then followed her.

The sharp pain in Lee's side almost stopped him in his tracks, but he made it to the woodpile before Miss

Dunn caught him. He fell and scrabbled away from her. His hand touched the rough, rusted blades of the shears Gareth had left there. He lifted them in warning, and she smashed them out of his hand and kicked him.

The kick sent a wet pain through his ribs and he tried to back away from her, then curled up to protect himself from the blows. A figure loomed out of the darkness behind Miss Dunn. Mr Leonard bent down. Rose up with the shears.

Miss Dunn was still kicking at Lee and didn't notice the blades as they bracketed her neck.

Mr Leonard's arms clapped together and the blades bit into her neck. She dropped to her knees then onto her face, the shears standing upright. The moonlight glistened around her as she bled. Mr Leonard stretched out a hand to Lee. After a moment he took it and Mr Leonard pulled him onto his feet, then sat himself down on the woodpile as Lee ran for the front garden.

"Wait," called Lee. They couldn't go to the police now.

Lee could hear the children on the road. Only Gareth was still there, waiting for him with one foot inside and one foot outside the gate.

"Call them back." Lee slumped to the ground, only noticing now that he was covered in Dunn's blood.

Gareth didn't understand, saw the blood, and tried to help him stand. "Dunn—" he said.

"Dead! And Mr Leonard..."

Gareth looked around.

"I think it's okay," said Lee.

Sixteen

ONLY THE LAST of the musty potatoes and some buttermilk were left. Josey took Siobhan and Teal into town. In the shop she handed a note to Mr Guigan. It was signed by Mr Leonard and requested the delivery of meat, milk, cheese, tea, sugar. Thanks to a generous donation, the delivery was to be repeated on a weekly basis. Mr Leonard was currently away. All enquiries should be directed to Josey who was nearing her majority and training to work at the orphanage once she had done so. They arrived back at the orphanage in Guigan's van. The gate was wide open and everyone helped bring the supplies in. Ross and Enda cleaned the Aga stove and brought in wood from the pile.

After they had eaten, Gareth and Lee dug six small graves under the alder tree for the dead children. Their names and ages were carved into the trunk. Miss Dunn's body was put in the hole in the centre of the Sick Room. The shed was emptied and the whole floor covered over with cement, a bag of which they found hardening in one corner. The lock was removed from the door and the light fitting repaired.

◆

Gareth had gone through the teacher's apartment with Josey and Lee. There was little of value in it. There were photos she had taken of children over the years, which they burned along with most of her clothes. The books were left, but her ledgers were also tossed into the flames. Nobody wanted to read what she had written, anyway. They did find a large red cash box with a snub-nosed lock in her wardrobe. The smallest key on the leather strap opened it. All the orphanage's documents were inside. The Children's Act, The 1933 Rules and Regulations on running an "institute for children's welfare," administration forms, funding requests as well as letters requesting donations, signed by Mr Leonard. There were pass books for two separate bank accounts. One for the orphanage. One for Miss Dunn. There was some money in the first one. There was more in the second one, if they could figure out how to get it. Her birth certificate and her application to work at the orphanage were there, which was a start. Although all the official documentation was addressed to Mr Leonard, there was no personal documentation for him in the box.

In the cavity in Mr Leonard's chest had been a yellowed photo of a smiling young woman with an older man wearing a wide suit.

◆

The children were used to working around the orphanage, anyway, so that's what they did. Gareth and Ross were able to work out how to run the boiler so that they could heat water for washing. Lee threw himself into teaching. He introduced science and maths. Everyone took to the lessons. Facts. Proof. Things that remained true, no matter what anyone said.

All the paperwork that continued to arrive was addressed to Mr Leonard. So, after cutting the yellowed photograph in two and putting the half without the woman back in his chest, they let him deal with it and he was installed permanently in the office. Donations were received with gratitude, requests to visit were regretfully declined. There were currently no children available for a placement outside the home. Siobhan could not be placed without Teal. Ross was learning a trade. Josey wanted to continue working at the orphanage. Lee was recovering from a distressing situation. Gareth was quiet and respectful, but too old for most people to seriously consider.

Nobody enquired after Miss Dunn. And the children looked after themselves.

Dive Into The Lonely Ocean!

Everyone's the same... on the outside.

"People Skins Volume I"

Get People Skins Volume I when you sign up to my newsletter full of stories, tips and reviews. This collection includes:

"The Lonely Ocean" – A family trip to rain-lashed Drumgorm? Worst holiday ever. And that's before, Meredith discovers the town's terrible secret.

"Teethgrinder" - Sean needs a dentist: you don't make it in Hollywood with bad teeth. His dentist has other needs.
And three more stories!
Go to www.morgandelaney.info/peopleskinsınewsletter to get it now!

Author's Note

I hope you enjoyed this story.

I hope even more that Lee, Josey, Gareth, Siobhan, Teal and the others—even Ross and Noreen—can turn "the Lamb's Home" into the place it should always have been.

The story was inspired by a bad dream, which formed the bulk of Chapter 1.

Chapter 16 was an attempt to re-create the feeling of relief I had on waking from it.

Only giving the children two names ("Ivan" for the boys, and "Anna" for the girls) was part of the dream. It made the story harder to write but made sense to keep: It's easier to mistreat people if you deny them their humanity.

Several characters sprang directly from articles and reports, including Ross, Noreen, and the well-meaning but useless Coltons.

Miss Dunn's abuses are a fictional representation of various reported abuses.

Mr Leonard, as nominal head of the orphanage, does nothing for far too long. Based on many, many reports.

Due to the scope of the inquiry the reports from the Irish Commission to Inquire into Child Abuse are a good starting point if you want to find out more about institutional abuse.

The Commission heard from over 1,000 witnesses of abuse in secular and religious institutions.

The Commission's Report was not allowed to include calls for prosecution or sanction of anyone involved as part of its recommendations.

http://www.childabusecommission.ie/rpt/pdfs/

About the Author

Morgan Delaney is an Irish writer of dark and fantastic fiction. Like other great Irish writers, Morgan prefers to live abroad. "People don't realise how vicious leprechauns really are," he explains.

He has lived in Ireland, Germany, Australia and Kazakhstan, and worked, among other things, as a building engineer, until one day, while he was writing a particularly outrageous cost estimate, the wind changed.
And he has been stuck like that – writing lies – ever since.
His favourite film is Terry Gilliam's Brazil.